<u>Daddy Cool</u>

About the author:

My name is Anup. I'm from Kerala state, India and had worked in software field for 11 years.

This is my first attempt to write a book and so I need all your blessings.

I would like to thank my family and friends for their continuous support. Hope you all will like my first novel.

This is a fictional story of a person who gets temper so easily and showed us that we should never be like him in life. He was successful initially in his life but due to his arrogant and harsh behavior and unnecessary self-pride, his life and career got destroyed. So here are some of the chronicles of his life.

Chapter 1: Childhood days

Keshavan was born in a village to a rich and reputed landlord family. His father even though headmaster of school by profession owned acres of land which he got from his ancestors. His father had a high value in society. His mother was house wife and was also from rich and reputed family and she too had acres of land. His father was somewhat angry person but was good at heart. May be Keshavan got this angry behavior from his father but his mother was very cool. They had 3 boys and 3 girls. Those days during 1950s it was very easy to live with just agriculture as livelihood Keshavan has a wonderful childhood with brothers and sisters. He was not good in studies and always used to play football with friends. Since his parents were landlords he thought why to study as they can live happily. During those days the importance of education just started in India.

Even though landlords' parents asked Keshavan to study hard because with just land they can't live in future. Time was changing and with just agriculture alone no one can sustain in life so the importance of education and job came in front. Only if we have good education then only, we can get good job and can settle down. So, parents asked Keshavan to study hard and get good job. But he was not good in studies and so he got very less Mark's. Teachers used to say that he was very bad at studies and will be very difficult to pass. But by luck or somehow, he managed to pass 10th exams. Now he needs to decide which stream he wish to take in pre degree and Later in degree so that he can get a good job.

But he was so weak in studies that he can't even decide which to select. Now this time his elder brother came to help him who was very good in studies. So, his brother sat with Keshavan and taught him all things required to get good Mark's in pre degree and later in degrees as well. So, it was his elder brother who made him an engineer. Later in life the funny thing was that he used to lie to his children's that he single handedly passed engineer exams and he used to get 100 Mark's in math's paper. The funny side is that he never got good marks in Math's and sometimes he even got zeros also. We know that some seniors use to blabber a lot that they did like that, this... etc. in their young life and that is a common thing not a problem but like how Keshavan exaggerated no one in this world would have done.

With the help of his brother Keshavan finally passed engineering exams in good Marks. He then came to cochin to pursue a career. At that time to get a government job was so easy, not like nowadays where we have to write entrance and PSC exams. But he doesn't like to work under a person and so he decided to start a new office of his own. He took some money from his mother and started new office in the city. Time flied and he became a successful engineer as not many engineers was there in cochin that time. He was one among the two successful engineers in cochin. So as time flied, he became successful and at the same time self-arrogant too. He built lot of hospitals and buildings in that city and became a reputed engineer.

Chapter 2: Success in life

His wealth got increased and he bought an ambassador car which was very rare in cochin that time. He got married to a village girl named veena and got settled in that city. Veena was so innocent that she obeys her parents like anything. She was not much educated and so she does not have any knowledge on what's going around the world. So same way she obeyed her husband also like anything. Whatever the husband says she used to believe as it is and whatever he asked to do she will do at once. As wealth increased Keshavan self-pride also increased which I will tell while going thru his life.

After marriage he took his wife to his parents' home. Initially it was very good time there but later problem started between his wife Veena and his mother. Even though she looks innocent she had a bad behavior inside seeing stupid and bakwas serials and so she thought that her mother-in-law also will be cruel too. It was just small issues like while she was eating food, she took curry with right hand etc. and that time mother-in-law use to mildly scold and sister in laws also used to make some fun out of that. But when Keshavan heard it, he took it so seriously that as an insult to his wife and all etc. So, he flighted with his parents and sisters and then left the house. Later when he became dad, he used to say to his children's that he loved his parents and had taken care of his parents like anything but the truth was that for small reasons he had left his own parents. Sometimes truth is really different than what we think or see. He then moved to his wife's family house where her parents are there. Here people used to say it's really a cheap thing to stay with wife's house as normally husband used to stay in his parents' house after marriage. But for a good life it's best to stay in our own house rather than in wife's or husbands, then it won't affect both sides. Anyways it's just beginning of story. Her parents were really good to him and he didn't had any problem living there with wife's parents. Her father was very old and after some days her father passed away. Her mother stayed with them till they had their children's and later she also passed away.

Keshavan developed as a builder in cochin and his office got expanded. It was very good time for him as he earned lot of money. He bought an ambassador car as mentioned earlier which was rare that time in 1990s in cochin. He became a father of two sons and was happy in life. He sends his sons to the most reputed school of the city. He planned to build his own house in his own land which was given by his parent. So, he was rich, happy and were going pretty smooth in life

His parents had given him 10 acres of land much before his marriage. He used to say later to his children's that his father had happily given the land. But don't know whether he took it cunningly or really parents had given only god knows. Later from his greed towards the land we can understand that he might have taken it cunningly from his parents.

Chapter 3: Problems started

As life was going smoothly, one day he got in a small argument with one contractor in his site and work got stopped. He at once gave case against him instead of trying to solve the problem and that's the point where problem started coming in.

Even that work gone still he had other works which was going fine. But his nature of quarrelling with others for simple reason never ended and it led to more problems on career side. Side by side he was more concentrated on the land he had which I had mentioned earlier. He thought of building a farm house on that land and so he appointed one person to take care of that land and also to cultivate coconuts, arecanuts, mangoes etc. All the money he got from his work he started investing on the land for agriculture purposes. But there was no profit from agriculture because he was not doing that for business purpose. So, if he was not doing agriculture for business purpose then why he invested that much money into it. This was the question which all his friends were asking. So, on one side there were so many cases that he had put against persons whom he quarreled while working and on the other side the money he got from hard work was unnecessarily wasting it in land. Lot of money he wasted on the land to buy agriculture products and also to pay salary to that person who was there to take care of land.

Keshavan even though had these many lands, used to stay with wife's family. They were staying in cochin city in a housing colony. One day he got in an argument with neighbors and the problem was that he used to play music in tape recorder very loudly and so it was very disturbance to the neighbors and so they asked to reduce the volume. But Keshavan got so angry and started fighting with them. He could have simply reduced volume or could have talked to the neighbors very calmly (as it was his mistake only) but he at once started quarrelling with them by trying to justify himself. This angry behavior created a very bad impression among neighbors and so they stopped talking or mingling with Keshavan. This also created a lot of enemies on neighborhood and as a result his family suffered a lot from neighbors. Keshavan's family couldn't do anything as he won't listen to anyone. If he says this neighbor is bad then it is bad only and will tell his wife not to talk to them. Poor veena she never dared to question him and so she obeyed him in this matter also. Keshavan told his children's not to play with relative's children as they are very bad people and will also make them bad. So as a result, they couldn't play with other children's and they really felt very sad.

Keshavan had problems with his and wife's relatives too. Both their relatives used to come to their home for gradual visits. They used to make fun of Keshavan and wife for the mistakes they in life and also blaming on matters like why fighting with neighbors, why not keeping the house clean etc. Keshavan and wife didn't like to hear these things from relative's and so slowly he and his wife started hating them. Gradually relatives stopped visiting Keshavan home.

The big fight with relatives came when Keshavan filed a case against his own relatives for a small portion of land near his 10 acres of land. Keshavan claimed that the two acres of land near to his land was his property and relatives had illegally taken it. Relatives said that it's their own land only and Keshavan is telling lies. So, they started quarrelling and instead of peacefully discussing with relatives he at once put case against them. All the relatives didn't like this behavior from Keshavan because Keshavan has already 10 acres of land, then why he needs these 2 acres extra. That is the greedy nature of human being, that even though they have enough wealth in hand still they need more and more and that's the same thing with Keshavan as well. The funny part is that he spended more money over this 2-acre land case than to his own family and after several years he lost the case so badly creating more loss for him than profit. All he gained was hatred from relatives and nothing else. His relatives never kept in touch with him in his entire life. This case later went for almost 20 years and it really shows how much greedy was Keshavan.

One day in midst of all these problems he did one biggest blunder in life. He took one home loan to build house in that land.House work got started and was going pretty fine. One day when Basement work was completed successfully, that old worker who was taking care of the land demanded some money from Keshavan (some 40000 Rs or so.). This Keshavan didn't liked as he never expected that his worker will ask this money in that situation. Even though he has enough money in hand he didn't liked the worker asking 40000 RS and so he refused it immediately and said that he can't give it now. That worker got angry immediately and went away. He later came back with some local party people and started quarrelling with Keshavan for money. This time Keshavan has to give money as it was party people and he can't refuse them.

From this point his bad time started. The house work got stopped soon after that incident but it was not because of just this reason that he had given 40000 to that worker, it was also due to the lot of debts he had as I said earlier. Lot of money, he invested in that land to buy fertilizers and also other agriculture uses. He had given lot of cases to whom he had flighted for simple reasons and now along with this curse from worker his countdown started. He could have discussed with that worker about his situation and could have avoid unnecessary fight with poor worker.

There was another funny thing that happened later, he had put case against a mobile company for a mobile not working properly but do you know the cost of it? ha-ha it was just 1000 Rs. He then spend thousands of rupees to advocates and courts to get claim of that. Who will do such non sense? He could have bought another mobile as it cost only 1000 RS. We can see a lot of people like that who fights for even 1 rupee. We can't take anything back from this world right then why??

Chapter 4: Family matters

These frustrations and angriness he started showing towards his children's also. His elder son is Ganesh and second son is Rahul. As typical father he thought to get fame and money thru his sons. He put a lot of pressure on children to study hard but Rahul and elder son Ganesh were average in studies and as a result it was difficult for them. So Keshavan send his children to tuitions so that they can study well. So, class plus now tuitions all together had put a lot of pressure on small kids and they rarely got time to play. It is really sad that in this world a lot pressure is given to children's over education and career. Childhood days are the best time we ever get to really enjoy in life and we will never get back those times thereafter. So, by giving pressure to children's we are not giving chance for them to enjoy their life and are doing cruelty to children.

Now apart from studies Keshavan got an idea to make his children a big star thru sports and the intention was to get fame thru his children's. Don't know from where he got these stupid idiotic ideas. If we want to earn something in life, we need to achieve it by ourselves and should never force others especially our children's or family to do it. Keshavan used to play tennis in his club and he started bringing his children's there. He got one good coach to teach his children's how to play tennis very well. Here the problem is that Keshavan put his interests forcefully on his children and that's really a bad thing. He should try to understand what children's really want and what are their interest. He should have asked them if they really want to play tennis or not? But sad part is that some parents never try to understand that, they simply want to implement their decision on to their children's and poor children's have to obey them, it is really pity.

His elder son Ganesh didn't have any interest in playing tennis and so for him it was really cruel while Rahul showed some interest and there was no problem for him. Anyway, playing is good for children that all knows but here problem is that their father Keshavan was always behind them watching them play. Keshavan used to watch their children's play and that felt very uncomfortable for children's. They were not able to play their natural game because always their father was behind them watching them playing all the time and used to scold and give unnecessary directions. Keshavan also didn't allowed his children to play with others. He will tell Ganesh to play only with his younger brother Rahul and used to say idiotic reason that other players won't be good guys and also don't share your skills to others. Which father will tell these kinds of things to kids like don't play with others and all? So due to this their game also didn't improved and this is really cruel. We should give freedom to our children to play themselves as we can see nowadays that certain parents accompanying their children's in Tournament and championships and it is really so cheap behavior I would say. How can they play freely? Off course parents worry about their children safety and all but for that they can pick and drop their children's when it is required but always going behind them will feel uncomfortable for them. Parents can watch them play and cherish them always but giving tension is not good that will affect their confidence badly. Children's have to play with others freely so that they can really enjoy the game and at same time learn how to play.

Comic or say tragic part in Keshavan case was that he used to show so much angry towards his children's. One day Ganesh was playing with Anil and Ganesh lost one match. Keshavan was watching this match and he got so much angry that he was literally jumping out of anger. All other players saw this behavior and got shocked. Keshavan took his children's from there and left via car. While driving he shouted so loudly at them and was hitting the break and accelerator hardly like anything out of anger. Due to their luck car didn't met an accident, that much forcefully he had kicked. Ganesh was so sad and frightened that we can't even imagine the situation he faced. It was as if India lost against Pakistan ha-ha really ?? common!! it was just a small game between friends and Keshavan made it like a hell as if it was a matter of life and death. This is what happens when parents put more interest on their children's activity rather than concentrating on their own work. We can't even imagine how much Ganesh and Rahul had to undergo from their fathers Keshavan harsh and ruthless behavior.

Keshavan wife veena used to see all these behavior from her husband towards their children's, relatives, neighbors and others but never tried to respond back as that was her nature. Woman that time won't even dare to enquire about their husband and they always obey and listen to them. That was time where Indian woman had to obey husband as taught by their parents. Now woman got liberated and started earning and now they all became independent and started questioning. So Keshavan children had to suffer as they didn't get any support from their mother veena.

Sorry got deviated towards his family life as I need to tell that aspect also. Now we come back to Keshavan professional life. As I said earlier his own house work got stopped due to the issue with that worker. After that issue his house work got stopped as funds were not there. So, he again started concentrating on his building works. He got some offers to build flats and started working on it. But he was not paying a single rupee as EMI on that house loan he had took to build his house. So that loan interest was getting increased day by day. Whatever he gets thru his work he was giving something to his family for sure but major amount he was still investing on that land again and again. So, with all these tensions coming up, he started a new habit of drinking alcohol to escape from all these tensions. The main mistake his parents did was that they gave acres of land much earlier in life that's why he became arrogant landlord else he would have really worked hard to earn money

Also due to his fight with other engineers and contractors for silly reasons he used to spend lot of money on cases, paying for advocates and courts, instead of discussing with them to solve issue. As I said earlier, he had his own office but later he had a small argument with office owner regarding office rent. Owner had slightly increased rent but instead of peacefully discussing with owner Keshavan got angry and quarreled with him. Owner then asked Keshavan to vacate office as soon as possible. Keshavan got angry and put another case against owner and then after few days he got permission from court to continue working there till case settles down. So overall cases which Keshavan gave and those which he got from others increased to more than 10. The problem with Keshavan was that he doesn't know how to talk peacefully with others, he always reacts in anger. Other funny thing as I already mentioned was that he had put cases against a mobile company for a mobile worth just 1000 Rs. He could have simply talked and solved these issues instead of quarrelling and there won't not be any cases.

Chapter 5: Poor children

Overall, he was in tension and he showed his frustration towards his children's while back home. One day he came to home and heard that his elder son Ganesh has failed in math's exam. After hearing this he was so angry that he shouted loudly at him and then he scolded and beated him. He throwed all the furniture's in the house and beated him so cruelly as if his child did some great mistake but it was just a small class test. He should leave all his office problems out of his house then only he can attain work life balance in life. This was a typical problem of a family man that they carry all their professional problems to their home and as a result it creates problem in home. So due to that his poor wife and children had to suffer.

He said to son that he used to get good marks in Math's but you failed in it so miserably how? this is really shame to me, how can I face society now? how can I tell this to relatives, it's a big shame to me etc. But the true fact is that as I mentioned early, even Keshavan was very bad in studies. He too had failed in math's exams so miserably but now see when he became old, he is saying lies that he got good marks. This was another problem with a typical family man that even though they had failed in exams during their childhood, they will never reveal the truth about their failure to anyone and in turn tell their children's that you have to get good Mark's otherwise it's a big shame to us. Also, another thing parent do now is comparing their children with neighbors or relatives' children. We can hear some dialogues like "see your neighbors or relatives' children's, they have got more Mark's than you, you also have studied the same thing then why you got less marks than him? you made me shame how can I look at others face?" etc. I wonder why people consider value over society more than their own children? why they take their children's matters into society as self-pride thing and why giving more pressure to children's during these young child days. Please let them be free, let them enjoy their childhood freely. Since Parents know that their childhood was best part of life then why they are not allowing their children to enjoy? they also know their childhood very well and know that it will never come back. We all wish if we can go back to our childhood at least once but we can't go right so let children enjoy. It doesn't mean we should allow children to do their own wish, no I'm not saying like that, we should have a control over them but at same time give some freedom also. More freedom can make them go in a wrong way and so some control and at same time allow them to play for a while at least.

The problem with Keshavan was not only the tension he had from his work but he has self-pride that he's coming from a reputed family and so his children should be best than others. Nowadays even in normal families too they started comparing their children with other children's so that they call tell others that their children are performing better than others. But poor children, they can't say anything as they can't raise voice against parents, all they can do is to listen to them and obey. I think some way children's need to raise voice as I heard in some foreign countries, that they have the law which says if even parents hurt their children's in any ways mentally or physically then children's have the provision to complaint against anyone including their own parents. I am not sure if its Canada or any other country but I heard that it's true and so I believe India should implement it strongly. Children's are future of India and all children should have the right to do what they wish. Children's should also have to freedom to decide which subjects to choose to study. India not only needed engineers and doctors, there are 'N' number of other opportunities here.

Chapter 6: Property is the main culprit

Coming back to Keshavan's life, still he didn't pay a single rupee to the house loan because he was still spending more on that land than on loans. He also had appointed another worker to take care of land for that stupid agriculture. Actually, he was not serious on the agriculture as it was just for time pass. The main agriculture items in that land were coconuts, arecanuts and few mangoes which he was doing just for time pass. If he was serious then he would have completely avoided other works and concentrated more on agriculture. Also, whatever he was getting from that land he was not selling it in good price. All I'm saying is he was having the land just to show others that he's the land lord that's it. So, if not serious then why he is wasting so much money. On a serious note, also, agriculture was not at all a profit business that time in India that's the sad part.

During the time of Keshavan's father it was not like that, with just coconut and pepper cultivated from that land they can live happily. That time cost of living was so cheap in India but now it is not like that, we can't live now with just coconuts and pepper. But much educated Keshavan still believed that he can live with coconuts and so invested a lot of money on that. I guess the hangover of feudalism from his father's times was left inside him and he wished to live like his father who was a respected landlord that time. His engineering works slowly got reduced a lot because more time he was behind cases and also on his children's education and sports. Morning time he will be with advocates and on courts and evening time behind his children's watching how they play and shouting at them. Sometimes he will leave his office work just like that and accompany children to tennis ground watching them play. Night time he will be boozing and that's what his one day is all about.

So, debt kept on increasing and after few years he got an idea to take more loans from other banks. Really don't know how but cunningly he took so many loans. Though he was rough and tough towards his family, he was very calm and clever towards others particular to the people he need money from and also towards clients that he needs to work. But those towards enemies and also towards those who doesn't like him, he was rough and tough. Cunningly he took so many loans, don't know how banks gave but he got in some or the other way. Banks slowly started asking why he was not paying any EMI but in return he gave case against bank saying that EMI calculation was wrong on bank side and also said other reasons as well. So, cases against bank also increased a lot.

He used to say to family that if he sells land then he no longer wills be called a land lord. Though he got it from fore-father's he thinks that it's his own hard earned one. Actually, that's another problem of land lords due to the land their self-pride increases and thinks they are king of that land but actually it was freely given by their forefathers. They don't know what's hard earned money is and they can't even show respect towards others. Keshavan can easily sell just 1 or 2 acres of his 11-acre land and can simply enjoy but his self-pride never allowed to do so.

Chapter 7: Interest in sports and pressure over education and career

He then thought to make his children famous by playing tennis. As I said earlier from somewhere, he got this idea to become famous via his children's achievements. He took his children far away from home to prepare for big tournaments. His first son Ganesh was not at all interested in playing tennis but Keshavan forcefully took him to play. He never keen to know if his son was interested or not. Rahul was somewhat Interested and after knowing that Keshavan started concentrating more on Rahul than Ganesh. He took him to big coaching camps and Rahul reached till district level. But Ganesh couldn't reach high level and so stopped playing tennis just before his 10th level exams. The reason is that if we pressurize anyone to do one thing in life it won't succeed ever, that's what happened to Ganesh, he was not interested at beginning itself to play tennis, then how come he can succeed.

One day some people from sports said to Keshavan that if he gives some bulk amount to certain people his child can reach Indian team. Actually, it was a trap by some fraud people to take money from him and by his luck he got to know about that and didn't paid any money to them. From all these incidents he come to know the dark side of sports and so finally he stopped going behind all these things especially going behind his children's forcing them to play tennis or any sports. Rahul on the other side continued playing tennis and with his own effort he reached till state level but later studies came in between and so had to leave playing tennis.

Keshavan by that time lost his office because the case he had given earlier against office owner lost badly. He had to surrender his office and his workers had already left him months ago due to his arrogant behavior. So, without his office he started losing his work. He again concentrated on agriculture but more than profit it was a huge loss for him. Though he got huge loss from land he still invested a lot of money there and now he has completely forgotten about loans. Suddenly cases started coming up one by one and so he had to spend a lot of money to advocates to extend the cases as long as possible. Comedy is that if he tries, he can clear all his debts in few days and he can be rich but the selfish nature of human to hold the land forever never changes.

Time flied away and now his children had grown up and passed out of school. Ganesh wants to start some business and so just wished to do a normal degree only but Keshavan wants his children's to be engineer or doctor. Keshavan asked Ganesh to take math's group in pre degree (plus 1 and 2 that time). Ganesh was weak in math's but he always obeyed his father and so joined pre degree in Math's group. One day he got one math's guide and using that he studied very hard. Due to his luck the same questions from that guide came and so he wrote exam brilliantly. One day exam results were announced and to know the results one had to go to the university that time. So Keshavan took Ganesh in his ambassador car to the university to know the results. Keshavan was so superstitious that time that on the way when car break down or when they got trapped in any traffic jam, or a black cat crossed the road then he got so disturbed that he felt that Ganesh would have failed in math's exam and that's why all these bad things are happening and so he then started scolding him all the way till university. Ganesh felt so bad after hearing all these negative things from father and he was so afraid thinking he might have failed. Although his exam was good and had the confidence of getting good marks still due to Keshavan's negative thoughts his confidence level got reduced. Finally, after a bad journey they somehow reached university and when they saw results, they got shocked to see that Ganesh got 100 Mark's in math's. Ganesh was so happy and danced in extreme joy. But on the other hand, Keshavan just said ok and started driving the vehicle as if he really wants his son to fail and he can scold him again. What kind of dad is he? at least he could have said good, at least one good smile, what will he loose if he appreciates. That's the nature of Keshavan the arrogant father and land lord, it's really pathetic.

After Ganesh completed his pre degree Keshavan pressured him to take engineering degree because he was an engineer first and secondly most of his family members had taken engineering or MBBS degree. So, it was a matter of prestige issue for him that in front of his relatives and friends, he wants to show that his sons are also engineer or doctor. Ganesh had to listen to his father because he was very afraid of him. On the other hand, Rahul never been into such problems because had gone to different places in the name of playing tennis and so he never got chance to listen to his father. One common thing seen in real life is that if a boy who's in home always being obedient towards his parents will be called a good obedient boy by society but in future when he faces the real-world during job or any such important thing in life then that time, he will struggle hard to adjust with the world. We need to mingle with society at least thru some friend's else children will grow up as a duffer i.e., of no use at all. Parents should allow their children to play and mingle with friends and society and that will make their children's more active in life.

Here Keshavan always controlled his elder son Ganesh. He used to scold him, sometimes threatens and make sure he won't play with other friends and instead make him study always. He used to say to him that if you want to play then play only with his younger brother Rahul else don't play with anyone as they might be bad children's Keshavan was saying   that if we play with other children's we will become bad person. Ha-ha sorry to laugh, he's saying as if he is very good, all society people know that Keshavan is the worst person of this society.

Chapter 8: Btech problems

Ganesh really struggled to get an engineering seat because his pre degree marks were average and he also had to face a lot of tensions from his father for getting admission in Btech.

Government used to conduct Entrance exam and there was an option system for candidates to select the college and branch stream which candidate which to join. So, Ganesh gave the list but he didn't get free seat and instead got payment seat down the order. So, it means he can join an engineering college under payment seat as of now and later if free seats are available then he can select that. So Keshavan got this point and asked Ganesh to join Btech under payment seat as of now in the hope that his son will get free seat later. Now in one-week entrance board asked Ganesh to join Btech in a college but since it's a payment seat he has to give a loan sanction letter saying that bank will pay the payment later or else candidate has to pay a bulk amount to college as it's a payment seat.

Now here the big problem comes for Keshavan is that as he was already in severe financial debts and so no banks will give him loan. Keshavan somehow wants his child to get admission into

Btech and so he met a manager who doesn't know much about his loans and then he got a confirmation letter that loan will be sanctioned later. With that letter finally Ganesh was able to join Btech under payment seat. Please remember here that Ganesh don't have any interest to join Btech but since his father was pressurizing him to join and also, he thought why to waste a year just like that as his father won't allow him to join a normal degree anyways. After few days of joining the college they asked Ganesh to pay the money as fees because the bank didn't pay the money to college which they agreed in confirmation letter. So, Ganesh went to that bank, meeting the manger to inquire about that. After seeing Ganesh Manager got angry and told Ganesh that his father Keshavan had taken lot of loans from other banks and he was in black list and so he can't give any loan to his sons as well. Ganesh was shocked to hear that his father had lot of loans as till now no one in family ever knew about it and he got so sad that how come he can continue his studies.

Ganesh went to his father and told the same thing what manager said to him. After hearing this Keshavan too got angry and said that we will see them in court. Now that's another case added to his list of cases. It was like Sachin getting another century and adding to the list of centuries he has, the same way Keshavan giving or getting cases and adding to the list of cases he has thus moving the list to half century. This is what Keshavan problem is, instead of solving the problem he just put cases against people. Keshavan believed that Ganesh still have a chance to get a free seat and then he may not need to take any education loan at all. But after few days entrance process got over but Ganesh didn't get any free seat. He told Keshavan that engineering allotment process was over and he will not get free seat here after. Another problem was that at this point they can't discontinue the course because in that case they won't get the surrendered original certificate back until the candidate pays the payment fees and complete Btech course. So, Ganesh have to pay whole payment fees and complete the course else he can't get original certificate back.

After hearing these things Keshavan got so angry and shouted loudly that Ganesh got frightened. It was really a scary scene. Keshavan at once raised in angry and started scolding Ganesh saying lot of things like it's because of Ganesh that they got in this trap and he had to pay the fees and now family is in danger, his prestige gone etc. and lot of other things which made Ganesh felt so sad that he even thought of committing suicide. It was very bad day for Ganesh and he really got so sad that he even thought to end his life. But due to his luck or goodness such kind of suicide thoughts left his mind else he would have really committed suicide because that much tension his father had created that we can't even imagine. Days past and Ganesh become normal hiding all his feelings inside of him. No one can imagine how much Ganesh suffered or gone thru those days. But he came to know more about father and also this was the point where he started hatred towards his father like anything.

If I need to tell Keshavan story then definitely his child Ganesh story also need to tell because most of Keshavan cruel things he showed was towards Ganesh only.

Ganesh was able to join Btech since Keshavan had put case against bank and also to college. Keshavan had given cases stating that he had given payment confirmation letter from bank to college and so after few days court ordered that Ganesh can continue his studies in that college till the verdict comes. Now Ganesh started his Btech studies but with half mind only thinking what will happen if his father didn't get any loan and couldn't pay money, how he can continue his studies then etc. He didnt tell any of his problems to his because he thought that his friends will never listen to sentimental things as they all come to college to enjoy. So, he was a silent guy in class and gloomy also. He couldn't concentrate neither on studies nor playing or mingling with friends because all the time he was thinking about fess he needs to pay. He though got few friends but really, he was alone and depressed. The intention of Keshavan was to make his children's grow higher in society and to regain the old reputation he had in society thru his children's and finally he was looking to earn money via his children. It is not a bad thing to regain fame or earn money via children's name. All parents wish the same and is a common thing that they expect that children's will earn money and take care of their parents. But it should be done by children's wish and not by force. I mean the education or job they do is to be by their own wish. If parents do it by force then it will be cruelty towards children and they won't succeed in life. Just think if our parents do same thing to us how we feel the same our children's will also feel. If children earn money their own wish, they themselves will give money to parents, no need to force or beg them.

Ganesh somehow completed first year in Btech but till now payment was not given to college. Since Keshavan had put case against college in court, university had held the first-year results of Ganesh. It means first year results will only come if Ganesh pays the payment fee for the first year. It was 1 lakh Indian rupee that time for Btech. Ganesh suggest his father to sell certain portions of land but Keshavan got angry and said it is easy to sell but to gain a land is difficult. It is true but when a crisis comes, they should sell the property right else what's the use to have all these property or gold in hand, it is meant to be used in crunch situations right. Due to these Ganesh had to face bad behavior from principal and teacher for not paying payment fees. One day he was not allowed to sit in class saying that he didn't pay the fees and so he can't sit in class from today. Lucky, they told these things to Ganesh only in principal room and so his friends didnt know these things but Ganesh poor guy really got upset now and thought how he will pay the amount and if he can't sit in class then his attendance will be an issue and also portions, he will miss.

After few days due to Ganesh luck, he got to know that his grandmother had some property which their relatives want to divide and share. But Keshavan's ego didn't allowed contacting their relatives to get the land share. So, Ganesh somehow convinced his mother and grandmother (mothers' mother) to take that land share. Somehow due to a lot of begging and plea from grandmother finally Keshavan agreed to get the land share. Keshavan actually allowed because first of all it's not his property (as said its grandmothers share) and second there is no land loss or money loss for him. He could have agreed at first place but since he didnt likes any of his or wife's relatives his ego mind said not to go in front of the relatives begging for that land.

After few days' grandmother signed the share agreement with relatives and got the land share. After that they sold land immediately and from the money, they got out of it they gave one lakh to college for Ganesh payment fees. After payment fees was paid Ganesh was able to sit in class and then after few days his long pending first year results were announced. He got some happiness after long time as results were released and in that he got only 2 arrears out of 10 papers and it was quite fine than expected. So, this shows us that if we try, we can solve our problems, the only thing we need is to look out for solution's. On the other side Keshavan got some money out of land but it was not of much use because that much huge was his debts. He still continued to take money from others and now there are mainly loans from banks and other resources like money lenders.

Keshavan thought let Ganesh complete Btech and then after that when he gets good job, he can ask him money to finish his loans. What a cunning father he is !!he's waiting for his son to pay his debt what a cruelty again! Ganesh then got some control over his studies after that but for upcoming years also they need money. This time Keshavan again went to some unknown bank and got one education loan. That time it seems civil score was not much considered while giving loans so that's why Keshavan kind of people got escaped from that and was able to get education loans and all other loans. That bank doesn't know many loans Keshavan had in other banks. So, Ganesh didnt had any problems with money during remaining 3 years in Btech. But now Keshavan's all expectations were now on Ganesh that he will repay all his study loans and also Keshavan's personal loans as well. Keshavan was thinking if his son get job in multinational software company then he will get very good salary and can settle all the debts. During that time IT was gradually booming in India and rumors were spreading that IT field will give more revenue than any other jobs.

Chapter 9: Life after Btech

Ganesh managed to pass Btech but got average marks only because he was not interested in it. By force if we pressurize our children to take Btech or MBBS they will pass for sure but won't get good marks and will not be successful in that field. After Ganesh passed Btech he then struggled very hard to get IT job.

During that time when Ganesh was not getting job Keshavan used to give tremendous pressure on him to get a job. But Ganesh didnt get anything not even cleared the first round of aptitude test. Keshavan started scolding Ganesh saying that due to him only he's in tremendous debt and life is in danger. But as we know it is Keshavan's fault that they are having these many debts but what to do parents usually blame their children for their own mistakes. His second child Rahul didnt dared to take Btech because he knew his father behavior very well as he had Seen what his brother had gone thru and so he purposely got less Mark's in engineering entrance exams so that he doesn't get into Btech course. He never stayed with father also that's why he became a brilliant child not like his brother who is innocent always

One day Keshavan told Ganesh to join engineer college as lecturer since he was not getting selected to software industry. But Ganesh was not even interested in lecturer field. His actually interested was in business like doing something on his own. But his father Keshavan always forced his interest on to his children's and never care or even listen to what his children wants to say. So, he threatened Ganesh to join college as lecturer. Ganesh got frightened and he prayed to god to somehow escape from this. Next day he got a call from friends saying that an MNC company is coming to college for recruiting. Ganesh got this as a chance to escape from joining as a lecturer. So, he attended the interview and at the end of day by his hard work and luck he cleared all the rounds and finally got selected into software industry. Keshavan was happy but never shown his happy face towards others especially to his children's. Keshavan was always strict because he thinks as a father, he should be strict else, he can't get control over his children's plus he will not get respect from others. As per me this is really a bad behavior, we should be friendly with our children's because if we are arrogant towards them then later in life children in turn won't love us and will always have hatred in their minds.

Meanwhile Ganesh was working in Bangalore Keshavan used to ask a lot of money. Since Ganesh was afraid and obedient, he immediately used to give him the money. But Keshavan never paid back any loans using that money. In fact, he used that money for paying fees to advocates and pending office rents. He was still trying to get more loans and using one loan he pays another loan, like that it goes on. He has land but it has already been modgaged and so he could not do anything. He can still find a buyer and discuss with bank to settle but his arrogant and feudal mind didnt allowed to do so as he thought once land goes from him then he would not be called a land lord, a typical land lord mind as they never sell till their last breath.

We can see a lot of poor people around us who doesn't have any land of their own and has to sleep on roadside but this Keshavan kind of feudal people always keeps their land till their last breath. It feels sad for his children's that they even they couldn't enjoy the land property. Keshavan situation was so pathetic that he has to borrow money to get food, yet he is still not even thinking of selling the property. His wife never dared to ask him because she was so innocent that she always used to consider him as god and so did not even try to question him. Children's were afraid of their father and so they also didnt dare to question.

Keshavan goes to his land rarely now but whenever he goes, he goes as if he is a rich land lord just to show workers that he's still the land lord but workers now adays very rarely comes and that too only when Keshavan asks to come. Now adays cultivation was nothing much there, it has just a few coconut trees and mangoes but the problem with Keshavan is that even in this bad situation he is seeing this agriculture as time pass not as a business. He should have either considered agriculture as his main business or he should have really concentrated on his engineer work but focusing on both together at same time, nothing got worked and finally both got collapsed. Here it is like some sayings that if we travel in two boats at same time with one leg on each boat then obviously, we will fall down.

Chapter 10: Fight to survive

Ganesh worked for some years in software field but still he was not happy with the work because IT field was really difficult to work on and also, he didn't have much interest on it so he found very difficult to continue the work. Software industry work seemed to be tough for him and so he thought since his father have some land why can't he start some business there or sell it to start a new business but he knew that his father won't allow and so he continued concentering on work.

One day when Keshavan called Ganesh for money he asked him why he need this much money now? and for what purpose he need? Somehow this time he got some courage to ask his father directly. After hearing this from Ganesh, Keshavan as expected got so angry but was shocked to see that his son first time dared to ask him. He took a deep breath for a while and in reply he said that he need money for some purpose. He cooked up some stories and told Ganesh. But the biggest thing Keshavan said was that due Ganesh's loan only he's in debt situation and so he has to clear his education loan first. Then Ganesh said why can't we sell some portion of property and then all the debt will be cleared in one go and also, we can start new business with the remaining money. For that Keshavan shouted loudly in anger and said that he can't sell land now as it is for their future purpose and also told Ganesh to concentrate on work and pay his debts first. He asked to give few moneys as of now from Ganesh as debt and even though he was sad he gave that amount from his salary. Ganesh salary was less only as he has just started his carrier only and also work was so difficult that anytime he can quit this job. Office problems he never told to his father as there is no use of saying because his father never gave time to listen to his children's problems, he just need money that's all.

After some months Keshavan again asked some money from Ganesh and this continued for some years. Keshavan used to say that he will return the money back but never do so. Initially Ganesh gave thinking it's the responsibility of the child to help father. But father should also understand his child's situation as well. He should understand how much Ganesh is earning, what all are his expenses and mainly is he happy in work. But Keshavan never cared of his son and he just say to him to work hard and its duty of child to help parents in any situation. Actually, Keshavan used his children's money to pay advocates for his court cases, to invest on agriculture which is of no use I said earlier and at last to booze to forget debts. Poor Ganesh in fact don't know these things he just gave money to his father and in return Keshavan never says thanks also and sometime just scold also when he didnt get money in time. Society will always tell people to take care of their old parents in any situation but won't check if parents are really taking care of their children's especially youngsters. If parents are taking money from children to booze or for long pending court cases, or any reason it is not an issue, society never cares it and just tells children's always to respect and obey parents. It's really sad that no one sees the effort taken by children to earn money. Why can't they understand that? Another thing was that Keshavan used to booze and when he come home, without talking he used to sleep, angry behavior he used to show only during rare cases and it feels that anger was coming from mistakes done by children's but real fact was that the anger was sue to reason that he was boozed and couldn't control anger.

Ganesh decided to somehow adjust in software industry until his education loan get over. So, for that he had to reduce his expenses and so he reduced. Then he started re-paying his education loan slowly and during this time whenever his father asks money, he would say that he can't give money right now as he need it to eat food and also to pay hostel rent where he is staying. After that Keshavan used to pressurize a lot to get money from his son but Ganesh never gave him any money and finally since Ganesh was not giving money he stopped asking and started hating his son. After some years of hard work one day Ganesh re-paid all of his education loan. It was not an easy task to finish the education loan because on one side his salary was very less and on the other side, he had his own expenses plus he had to take care of his family's expense too as there were no financial help from father. There were a lot of Relatives from mothers' side as well as fathers but no one helped because Keshavan had cut short all the family relations as I said earlier. So, Ganesh was really happy that without any one help from anyone he cleared all his education loans.

Chapter 11: truth revealed and after affects

Ganesh proudly told dad that he has cleared all his education loans. Keshavan got surprised that his son has cleared his education loans within a few years. But he just said good only and he was not really happy. Now slowly Ganesh started noting why is he still not happy when education loans are finished, is there any other debts he had? So, with the help of his friend who is a bank officer, he started investigating. During this period in India PAN card got mandatory to whoever has financial assets and all our financial dealings, be it investments or loans, all details get recorded with PAN. So, using Keshavan's PAN card which he took secretly he asked his friend to get all the financial details of his father. Finally, after some days Ganesh got all the details of his father's debt and after seeing that he got really shocked. He then told this to his mother and brother that their father has these many loans. Also, one day when Ganesh was in home, he got a letter from bank via post and he got a chance to read it. So now family came to know all the debts Keshavan have. Same thing for boozing too Keshavan wife saw when he was hiding beer bottle in backyard.so now all secrets of Keshavan are revealed to his family. But it was too late now, if they had found it earlier then it would had been very good to the family. Ganesh brother Rahul too meanwhile had got job.

One day Ganesh got courage to ask his father how come this much loan and cases came up. This shocked Keshavan as till now his family never came to know these details, because he was hiding all details from them. Then Keshavan said a blunder that debts are due to Ganesh's education loan. Ganesh really got angry and he said why you are ways blaming me? He again said that I already had paid my education loans and he showed loan closing letter to Keshavan. After that Keshavan had no words and kept silent for a while. But Ganesh didnt leave the matter and he again asked how come these many loans. Now Keshavan replied that all debts are due to the expenses in bringing up his children's. Ganesh replied that "Common what a non-sense!!! You were a successful engineer that time and had earned a lot of money and now you are saying this bullshit and stupid thing that you took loan to bring them up? Why you are you telling such a big lie". Actually, Keshavan was saying these blunders to deviate from what family was asking, basically he don't want to reveal how these many loans came. Now even he got angry but Ganesh stood firm on the question as he was not afraid anymore. Life will show us one day that there is no need to be afraid of anything. Normally children's and youngsters are mainly afraid of everything because of the concern for the future. Concern are over mainly whether they will pass in exams, whether they will get good job /good salary or whether they get good girl for marriage. So, once we get mature in life, we will realize that there is nothing in life to get worried off then why to be afraid. Off course we still need money and that concern will be there for life time but that's the part and parcel of life. For Ganesh case now there is no need to be afraid of parents as he had gone thru all the hardships and understood that there is nothing to worry about it.

Now coming back to Keshavan reply. He had said that these many debts are due to expenditure of children's i.e., to take care them, to educate them, and mainly money was for the Btech payment. Ganesh replied "how come? he only had paid most of Btech loan and remaining money was taken by sclling his grandmother land, then how come?". Ganesh replied boldly all these things and he also said that "even his education expenses won't cause this much debt then how come this much debt came? Keshavan got really angry and said that all are lies and was saying something stupid bakwas things which was not at all related to the matter Ganesh was asking. This was the start to the problems in family. Now since family came to know all debts and cases Keshavan had then lost his image completely. He has now lost the power of family head and he started escaping from their question and from the family itself.

One more thing is that Ganesh was trying to look for good marriage proposal but he was not able to find it. Keshavan was not even trying to search for a good alliance. Now Ganesh came to know why his marriage was not happening. It was because of his father's debts plus 'N' number of cases his father had in court. Who will give a girl to a family who has lot of debts and cases? Ganesh got very sad and asked father why he never bothered about his children's life. If not willing to get them married then why given so much pressure for their education and job, is it for money? Keshavan got tremendous angry and started quarrelling with Ganesh. He was not correctly replying to what Ganesh was asking but saying he had taken care of them when they were child and now children's questioning back is not at all good etc. This is problem with parents if children's ask something to parents then they will say that they had taken care when they were children's and skip the topic. Why? Main thing they say is that they had taken care of children's during childhood but its parents' duty to take care of their children's and they should not say later as if it's a big thing as such.

Ganesh tried to get some alliance on his own but his father did not agree to it. So many alliances gone just like that due to his father's rude and bad behavior and some due to the rumors about debts and loans his father had. Ganesh told his father to at least change his rude behavior and for that Keshavan got angry and said that his behavior is good only and other people behavior are utter waste. Ganesh laughed and said that this is like as if we are the only good persons in this world and all others are bad. No one will agree that their behavior is worst true!! but should realize themself that some problem is there to their family due to their behavior and should change as much as possible. Here Keshavan can understand and realize from his children's behavior and that of neighbors and relatives that some mistake is there in his behavior but what to do as people get old, they won't change their attitude. Also, it's difficult or can't change the behavior of old people because they won't hear anything from others. Some people used to say that we should never dare to advice old guys because they never listen to us but just give advice to others.

Chapter 12: love changes life

Ganesh was really sad and depressed that his marriage won't ever happen in life. But since life should go so, he started concentrating on work.

One day a beautiful girl named maya joined office. She was a Malayalee and Ganesh were working in a company where Malayali people were rare. One day she came to know that Ganesh was also a Malayali and so got introduced to him. Their friendship started growing slowly and Ganesh fall in love with her. But he was very shy person and so didn't had the courage to propose her. They used to discuss a lot of things, spend time together but he never dared to convey the love. After few months when Ganesh was on sick leave, she came to meet him and took care of him. Still, he was not sure if she really likes him or was it just friendship. One day she got mail from company that she will get transferred to Kerala soon and when Ganesh came to knew this, he felt so sad and for a few days he couldn't speak to her. Later one day she came to his cabin where he works and forcefully took him outside the office. There she asked with anger that why you are not speaking to me and avoiding me. Ganesh said that since he heard the news that she got transfer and will be leaving him he felt sad and that's why he couldn't speak to her as she's the only friend there. After hearing this she said that she too is sad to leave him but what to do its company decision and she have to obey. But she said that even though she goes away they can still talk over phone and meet once they get free time as that place is not that far away, then why to be so sad? Ganesh couldn't reply to that and was in gloomy situation. That discussion gone for a while and After that she came to know that this is not just friendship, its more than that. She came to know from Ganesh face that he was in love with her but his is afraid to propose. So, after some time they left from there. That night both were thinking of each other and couldn't sleep. Maya couldn't sleep at all as she too was in love with him and so she called Ganesh over the phone. She was shivering while speaking and took some time to say hi itself and then slowly she said that she feels something a unique feeling and couldn't sleep.

Ganesh was in shock state after hearing that from Maya and couldn't understand what's happening. After few seconds he got the feeling that that she too loves him. He knew that its right time to say those magical words and so he finally said that he really loves her very much and can't live without her. Maya got so happy and she too said the same thing. That night was really the beautiful and romantic time of their life. They felt so much happy that they wish that the night never ends. Next day when they met it was like, what I can say about that moment's, can't explain that in words, it was the most beautiful moments to cherish their whole life. So, the love story continued and they loved each other like anything in this world and then the time came where they have to decide about their future. Ganesh want to marry her as soon as possible but how to tell his family problems to her. Ganesh decided one day and told all his family problems to her. After hearing all the problems, she said that it is not at all a matter to worry, she doesn't have any problem to marry him and said that they can talk to parents about marriage and if it doesn't work then they can go and marry in registered office but only thing she need is the promise that they will be together always, no matter if entire world will be against them. Ganesh after hearing this was overwhelmed with outmost joy ever in life and gave the promise that he will be always with her till last breath. He shared all his stories with her and Ganesh was really lucky that a girl who knows all his family problems got ready to marry him.

One major hurdle was that maya was from a different caste. When Keshavan heard that Ganesh is in love and also wish to marry a girl of low caste then he got so angry and said they will never agree to it. Ganesh this time got courage and asked "why they won't agree to their marriage? what's there in caste? we humans are all same why the difference why? ". He asked his father not to see her Caste and instead see maya's kind heart to accept Ganesh in spite of all their family debts and cases. Ganesh asked Keshavan that which family girl will be ready to marry him whose family has lot of debts and cases? But arrogant father Keshavan didnt heard anything from him and said that "whatever you say we won't accept a girl of low caste". He also said that debts and court cases are part and parcel of his feudal family but his family had and will never accept a low caste people. Ganesh got so angry and said to father "Due to these debts and cases only his life has gone and what you earned till now? due to these feudalistic mindsets only sadness and tension only they got till now. What kind of life are we living?". After saying this much, with much angry and sadness he left from there. This cast-based issue is one of the biggest problems still India is facing. So many lives were destroyed due to these caste-based issues. Why we differentiate ourselves over caste? why they don't have freedom to do they wish? Do any particular caste have a different thing in body no right then why certain caste people are not allowed to live happily why??, it's really sad. Ganesh also asked his mother's permission but he was heartbroken to see that her mother too said that they won't accept a girl of low caste. Ganesh tried to convince his mother by advising that now adays there is no differentiation over caste and all are same. But still his mother was adamant over the thing that she won't accept her at any cost. Then Ganesh understood that she always listens and obeys her husband and she won't go an inch against her husband

After certain months Ganesh still tried to get parents' permission somehow but after so many discussions also his parents never changed their decision and was stick to the matter that they will never accept a girl from low caste.

Chapter 13: Marriage

Ganesh got permission from Maya's parents as they don't have any problem with caste issue or the cases his father is having, they just want their daughter to be happy. They know that their daughter loves Ganesh more than anything in this world. They want to give everything to their daughter and so they were more than happy to give her to Ganesh and were ready to face any problems from Keshavan. So, Ganesh decided to marry Maya as soon as possible. After few months without Keshavan permission finally they got married. It was just a small function only with just maya's parents and some of their friends. It was the first victory of Ganesh as first time he did something bravely against his father. The Marriage was successful with the blessings from Mayas parents and after they had a small reception in a hotel where their colleagues from their companies were invited. After reception they went to Ganesh own apartment which he had bought earlier. Thus, they started their new life happily.

Keshavan came to know that the marriage was over and so he got very angry that he even said that he doesn't have any son named Ganesh and he's out of his family. This is the problem with Keshavan kind of people, they won't leave their caste values till last breath, no matter if its own child or anyone. That's the problem with how they being brought up. From the childhood they had seen this caste differentiation and feudalism from their forefathers and same way they too live with those ideals in their mind. Now time has changed and we youngsters should change it completely so that our future is bright and beautiful.

Keshavan before marriage itself had tried hard to change the mind of Ganesh to somehow avoid marriage. Keshavan even cooked up stories that Maya and his mother are really bad and he told Ganesh that Maya is not good girl and will cheat him one day in future. Keshavan told all sorts of bad things about maya and her family that I feel ashamed to talk about. How come a father can tell such things about his daughter in law? it's really a bad behavior. Ganesh felt so sad and angry that he based his father like anything. Maya told Ganesh that let them speak anything about them, it doesn't matter to her and asked Ganesh that "we know each other very well then why to bother about what others are saying". So, Ganesh kept his cool mind and started ignoring all such things. Keshavan still continued his efforts thru several ways in order to somehow make them get divorced. But Ganesh took firm on his decision as he was really in love with Maya and so all the efforts of Keshavan was gone wasted. He also tried talking with some big caste people and relatives to avoid the marriage but all that attempt got failed since that much hatred he had created in the minds of relatives and neighbors. Since it was south side of India Keshavan didn't went on a violence path else if it was north, he could have tried killing his own son also, that much cruelty is happening over caste. After marriage also he tried torturing both to somehow get them separated but since maya and Ganesh were in true love no one was able to break their relationship that much stronger was their love. Keshavan second son Rahul was seeing all these things done by his father and so he decided to go away from house to stay faraway from father and to concentrate on career.

After some time, issues got settled down as there were no more problems from Keshavan and so Ganesh and Mary lived happily thereafter. They both got job in cochin in it park and got settled there. Since Ganesh was not interested in software field he later after discussing with maya left the IT field and started own business. After much hard work their business got clicked and they both happily settled there. So, without any help from Keshavan Ganesh finally got success and happiness in life. It was all due to Maya coming to Ganesh life that he got a new happy life else it would have been really bad.

Chapter 14: Realization on verge of climax

Time flied away and after few years Keshavan and his wife felt so alone at home because both of their children rarely to visit them and that too to only talk to their mother. Now Keshavan stopped torturing Ganesh and decided to think that he never had any son in his life. His wife never dared to go against husband because as I said earlier, she was so innocent that they never questioned their husband and always obeyed and respected him like God. She never goes against husband even they do mistakes. I heard this quote somewhere that giving more respect or obeying more than a limit is a kind of slavery. The culture of obeying and respecting husband is very good only but what I'm saying is that more than a limit we should not be so obedient. Whenever we see bad thing in life we should at least react and should try to stop them, no matter if its husband, wife, parents, children's.

Time flied again and Keshavan started feeling the loneliness as there was no one in house apart from his wife. As I said children rarely comes but just to see their mother and never dared to talk or mine their father. Keshavan really felt sad for this kind of behavior from children's that they are not talking to him but still he was not ready to accept Ganesh and Maya. He was still adamant on that matter and he's still saying that he won't accept them at all. Now Ganesh also now never mind his father and was happily living with Maya. Despite all these problems in family Keshavan was still concerned over land property. He still never wishes to sell the property. Debt reached at maximum stage and cases was going to the last stage and was in verge of judgment.

Suddenly one day Keshavan decided to go for settlement against bank. Because he was afraid that he may lose the case and also, he wished to sell in order to enjoy now as children was never cared him and he need money to mainly booze. So now he decided to sell a small portion of land and so he went to bank for compromise. This thing he should have thought it and implemented much earlier when children were grown-ups but he was selfish that he thought he can use children's money for his expenses and to re-pay all his loan's, thus keeping the land safe in his hands. We can see how much cunning he was but never seen a father like that who never cared his children's. Children's heard that their father Keshavan is going to sell the property but this news didnt changed anything on their side and they said "if father sells land or not nothing matters to them as they don't want that property. They have their own hard-earned money and also they don't want a property which had only given sadness and nothing else in their life". Keshavan after hearing this didnt get sad and he said that he also doesn't care about his children's and that he will decide his own life. So, after some months Keshavan sold some portion of land using broker and all his debts were cleared. He was sad that some portion of land he lost even though 70% still there. How much greedy Keshavan was? But he need money badly to booze and also for the agriculture expenses and so he sold certain portions of the property. Time really flied and now Keshavan was happy enjoying in land. But at the same time, he felt so lonely as his wife had passed away few months before and so now no one was there with him as I told earlier that his children never liked to stay with father. They were living far away from city to take care of their family life.

Now Keshavan even though most of his debts and cases are over and he got his land papers without any debts, still he felt really sad because he was all alone now and loneliness is killing him each second. Now he finally realized that even thought if we have crores of money or acres of land but if there is no one to look after then what is the use of all these things. But now it is too late for the realization as he should had thought these years ago and now what's use of it as he and his family had already suffered a lot of problems. But even though it is too late, at least now he realized his mistakes and for the first time ever he decided to bring back his sons and daughter in law along with grandsons to his home. So, he planned to go one day to meet them and to mainly to say sorry for all the bad things and mistakes he did towards them and also to either bring them back home or to stay with them all his remaining life.

But... But... suddenly a major heart attack occurred to Keshavan. He felled down from the seat while watching TV. But in that 10 acres of land, he was all alone at that time. He tried to grab his phone but couldn't reach to it as it was kept very far away from him. He shouted loudly as he can but who will hear him as that much big was his land and home in center of it. After some struggles, he got unconscious and later he passed away. His body was laying down for more than 5 hours until some boys saw it while they came there to eat mangoes. Boys at once called local people there and they took Keshavan to hospital but it was too late, doctors declared that he was already dead. Keshavan's Sons came to know of this tragedy and rushed to hospital to see him. Even though they were angry but when tragedy comes all will forget everything. Keshavan was cremated next day and his sons were really sad as they couldn't meet their father before dying and also Keshavan was really a changed person now. That's what a life is all about, we can't say what will happen the next day. So better we enjoy every second of life instead of keeping worrying all the time thinking of money. If Keshavan was staying with his sons someone would be present at that spot and they could have saved him.

After some day's children were shocked to know that all the property which Keshavan was holding are now in his friends' name. One friend named Hareesh who he was so close with Keshavan during his last days cunningly took sign of him while Keshavan was in fully booze state and he got all property under his name. The children never cared of these thing as they never bothered over the land property because till now, they only got sadness from that property, all cases, debts were due to that, their lives are gone completely due to that and main thing is that they never got the love of their father.

This is what irony if life is all about, all his life Keshavan was behind that land property and now see the irony that after he passed away, he couldn't take anything from this world not even one hand of mud from that property to heaven. Forgot about property he couldn't take a single paise, that's the hard thing people will never realize. Keshavan might be thinking this from heaven that if he had at least given that property to his sons then at least the property will be with his own family instead of being with Hareesh that bloody cheater. People fight, loot and do anything to earn money, land or fame in society but can they take all these things from this world after death? No thing, right? as they can't never take anything from here not even one hair. But even people know all these things they do anything to live and that's the human nature.

So, this is all about Keshavan's life. This is purely a fictional story and have no resemblance to any person dead or alive. The name daddy cool is contrary to the character Keshavan as we all wish that we have a daddy that is always cool and lovable and not to be arrogant like Keshavan.

Daddy cool

Thank you very much for your patience

Thanks, and take care

Anup

Daddy cool